LARGER THAN LIFE

DEBBIE DADEY

Illustrations by SCOTT GOTO

Walker and Company
New York

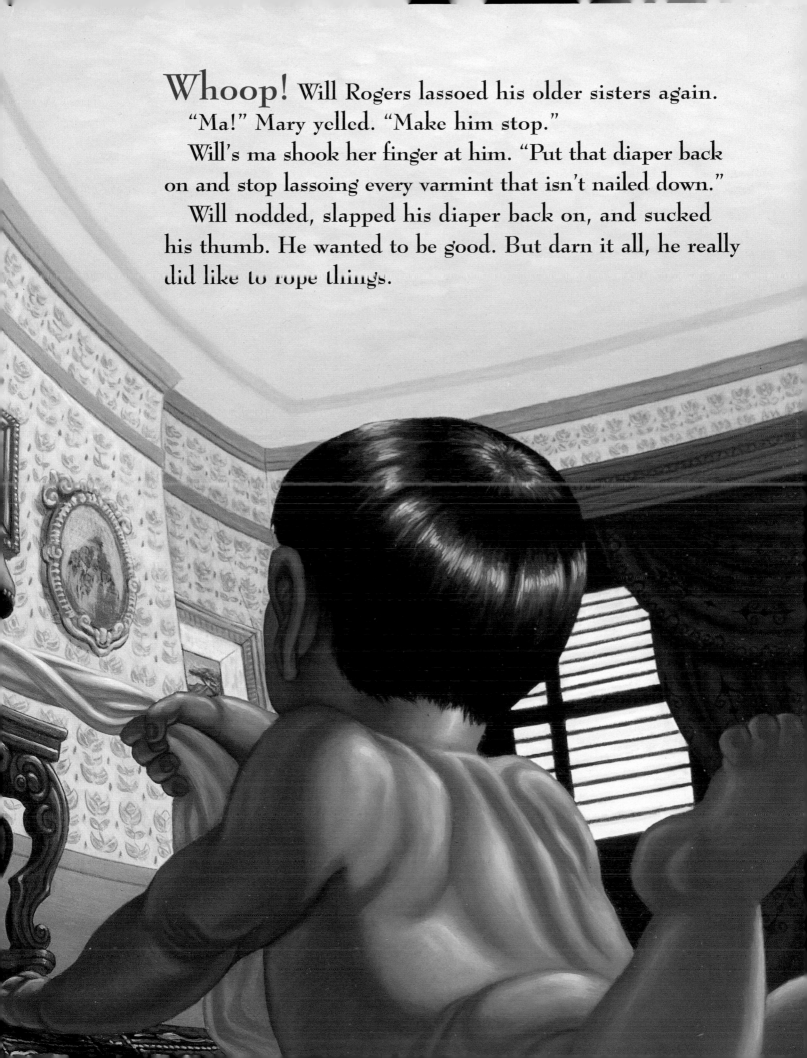

Whoop! Will Rogers lassoed his older sisters again.
"Ma!" Mary yelled. "Make him stop."

Will's ma shook her finger at him. "Put that diaper back on and stop lassoing every varmint that isn't nailed down."

Will nodded, slapped his diaper back on, and sucked his thumb. He wanted to be good. But darn it all, he really did like to rope things.

By the time Will was three, he could rope every steer on the ranch with one throw of his lasso, sling the whole passel of them over his back, and fling them into the corral.

The cattle were getting mighty bruised from all that roping and flinging, so when Will was five he was sent to school. He set off for town with a pencil in one pocket and his lasso in the other.

Will learned his ABCs, but during recess he roped every kid in the school, half the teachers, and even the principal's horse. Will's rope scared that horse so, it took off and dragged him halfway across Indian Territory. By the time the horse stopped, Will had plowed up three hundred acres of prime farmland with his feet.

That principal was whopping mad when he saw his horse sweating something fierce. "You get," he told Will, "and don't come back until you lose that lasso."

Will couldn't part with his rope, so he never went back to that school. He ate, drank, brushed his teeth, and even took a bath while practicing throwing a rope. His ma would have to come in at night and tear the rope out of his hand, or else Will would lasso every wild horse and jackrabbit within two hundred square miles and never even stop snoring.

When Will got older, he had what's called itchy feet. He didn't much cotton to farming, and ranching was just too easy, so he decided to see the world and have some adventures.

He traveled all over the world doing rope tricks and telling jokes to make people laugh. As a matter of fact, Will once got a crowd in Africa to laughing so hard they couldn't stop for a month. They laughed so hard their tears ended a twenty-year drought.

During his travels Will heard tell that the big city of New York was full of adventure, so off he went to see about being part of a famous Broadway show called the Ziegfeld Follies. The elegant Mr. Ziegfeld wouldn't even talk to a country bumpkin like Will, much less hire him, so Will signed on with a small Wild West show.

One day the show brought in a bull bigger than an army tank. Folks came from all around to see the bull that was so mean it practically spit fire. Trouble was that the bull broke out of its pen before the show even began, and charged straight toward the huge crowd.

Several cowboys tried to catch it, but the bull knocked them plumb silly. There wasn't anything for Will to do but twirl his lasso and drop it over that monster bull's neck, saving the crowd from certain death.

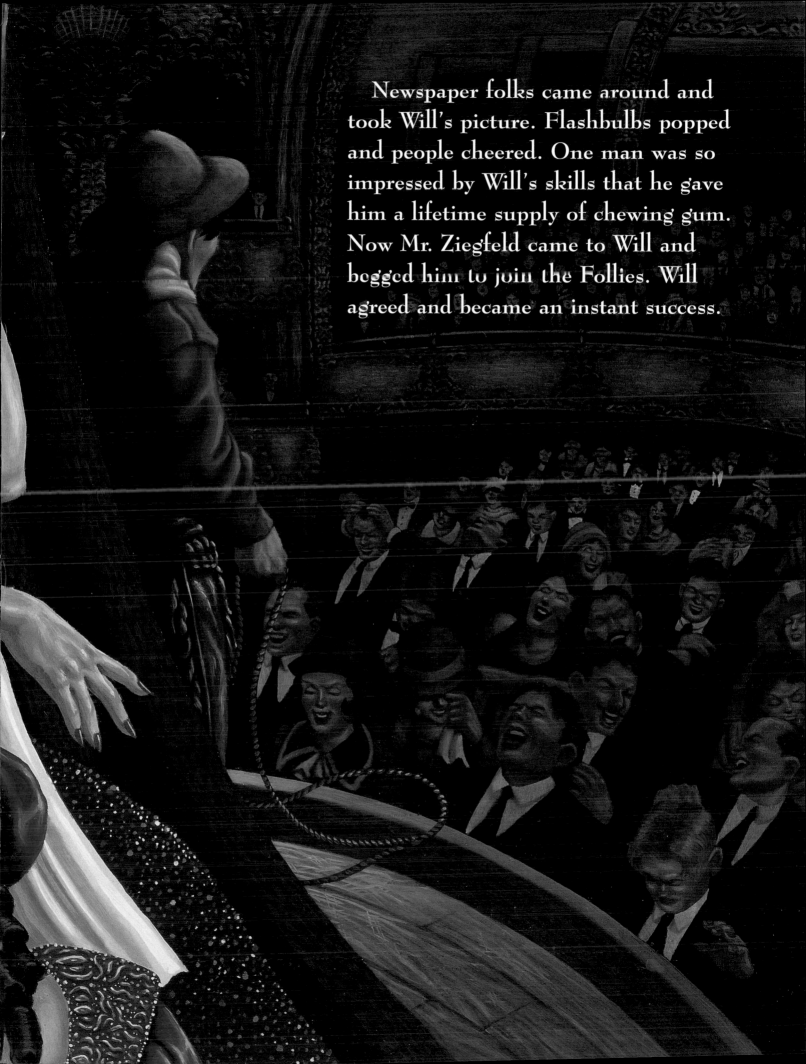

Newspaper folks came around and took Will's picture. Flashbulbs popped and people cheered. One man was so impressed by Will's skills that he gave him a lifetime supply of chewing gum. Now Mr. Ziegfeld came to Will and begged him to join the Follies. Will agreed and became an instant success.

When Will entertained an audience, he never used jokes made up by other people. He made up his own funny stories. He got ideas from reading newspapers. Will read every paper he could get his hands on to get one funny story. He kept a hundred kids busy delivering his papers. Will always said, "All I know is what I read in the papers."

Will was always busy, but he found time to marry his lifelong sweetheart, Betty Blake. "The day I roped Betty, I did the star performance of my life," he told his friends. Will taught his children to rope, ride, and play polo.

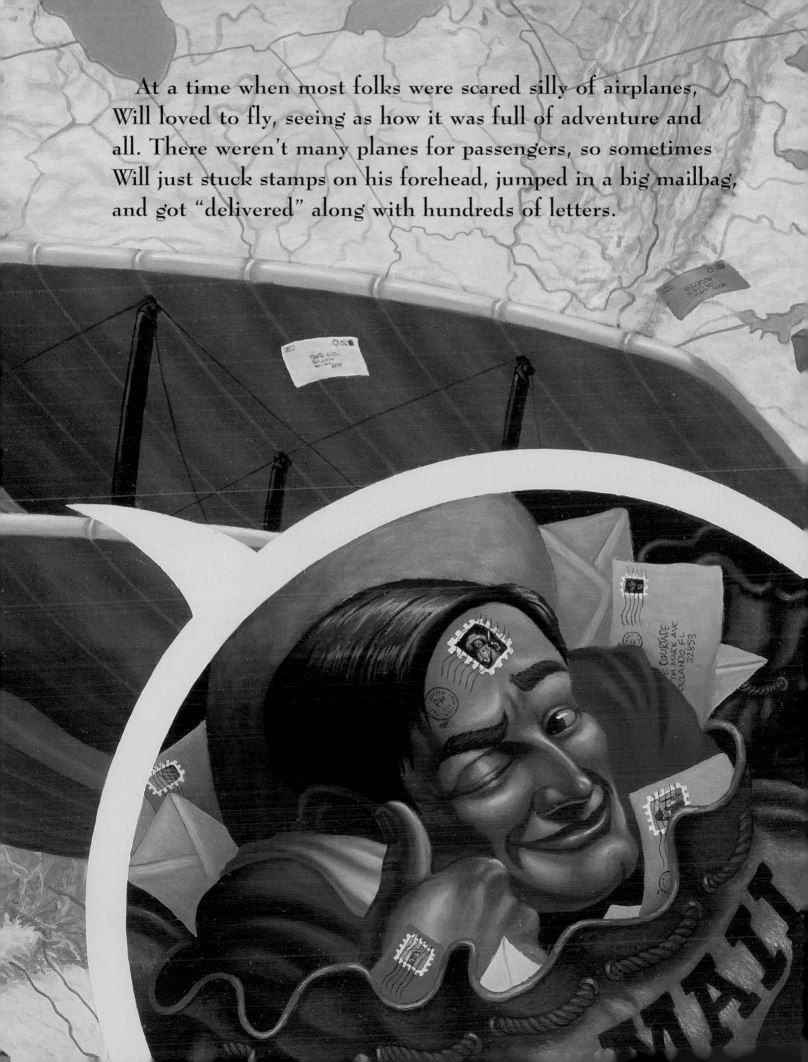

At a time when most folks were scared silly of airplanes, Will loved to fly, seeing as how it was full of adventure and all. There weren't many planes for passengers, so sometimes Will just stuck stamps on his forehead, jumped in a big mailbag, and got "delivered" along with hundreds of letters.

Will was prouder than punch the day he got to meet the most famous pilot of the time, Charles A. Lindbergh. Lucky Lindy was the first man to fly nonstop across the Atlantic Ocean. Will went to Mexico with Lindbergh on a goodwill tour.

Will got the folks in Mexico laughing so hard they durn near fell off the end of the earth. Will was quick, though. He pulled out his lasso and did the hardest trick of all, the Big Crinoline. He made a huge circle over his head with his ninety-foot-long rope. The circle got bigger and bigger till it surrounded the whole crowd. Then Will let the rope drop. He caught the entire bunch of people in his lasso before they even had a chance to holler for help.

Lucky Lindy was mighty impressed by Will's roping. "Why I bet you could rope the whole earth," Lindy told Will.

"I reckon I could," Will said, scratching his head. "But the hard part would be getting the rope back."

"Just leave the rope around the middle," Lindy suggested. "It'd be a good way for pilots to tell which half of the world they're in."

"By gum," Will said, "I'll do it." Will had to go to every country to collect enough rope, but finally he was ready. Lucky Lindy and folks from every town in Indian Territory gathered around to watch.

"Stand back," Will told Lucky Lindy. "This is gonna cause one big wind." He wasn't kidding. When Will started whipping that huge rope around his head, every chicken in the whole world had its feathers blown plumb off, and road signs in thirty countries were wiped clean of their writing.

It took every ounce of strength that Will had, but he threw that rope all the way around the earth and pulled it tight. The earth jerked him plumb out of his boots and skyrocketed him to Mars. It looked like Will was a goner, but he hung on tight. He swung back to earth and dug in with his heels. He hollowed out a little gully folks started calling the Grand Canyon. His feet were a might sore, but that didn't matter to Will. He'd done it! He'd helped out all the pilots. Lucky Lindy slapped him on the back. "Let's call that rope the 'equator', because there's nothing to 'equal' that trick."

Of course, Will was a hero, what with saving those people and making the equator and all, and there wasn't anything to do but make statues and name roads after him. It was all a might embarrassing to Will, so he decided to have another adventure. He took off in a plane with a feller named Wiley Post who liked adventure as much as Will. Rumor is that they're still up there, flying around and roping the stars.

THE TRUTH

Although a lot of this story is exaggeration, William Penn Adair Rogers really was born on Election Day, November 4, 1879, in Indian Territory, which is now known as Oklahoma. He told folks, "I am part Cherokee, and it's the proudest little possession I ever hope to have." He also said, "My ancestors didn't come on the *Mayflower*, but they met the boat." Will was the last of eight children.

The truth is that Will did learn to lasso when he was just a little kid. Uncle Dan Walker, a cowboy friend, patiently showed Will again and again how to throw a rope. Will practiced constantly on just about everything. On a dare, he even tried to rope the headmaster's horse. As a young man, he traveled to Africa and became the first person to lasso a wild zebra. Will really did save a crowd from a charging bull before joining the Ziegfeld Follies.

In 1908 Will married his lifelong sweetheart, Betty Blake. They had four children together.

Will liked to travel by airplane and often ended up going by mail plane. He believed in air travel at a time when very few people had

even seen an airplane. Will Rogers and Charles Lindbergh became good friends, and together they were goodwill ambassadors to Mexico.

In the time before television, Will gave lectures, wrote newspaper columns, and performed on radio shows and in movies. He read a lot of newspapers to come up with his funny stories, and his own column appeared in five hundred papers weekly.

During the Great Depression, in the 1930s, listening to Will Rogers on the radio was the happiest part of many people's day. A lot of folks had lost their jobs and didn't have enough food to eat. Will gave benefit performances to raise money to help people down on their luck. He once gave up a half a million dollars in earnings just to help out a good friend named Fred Stone.

Will brought joy to our country and is still remembered as one of the funniest men ever born in America. "I never met a man I didn't like," is his most famous saying. Will and Wiley Post died in a plane crash on August 15, 1935. When news spread of Will's death, the famous singer John McCormack said, "A smile has disappeared from the lips of America."

In loving memory of my dad, Voline Gibson,
who grew up riding his pony in Uniontown,
Kentucky.   —D. D.

For my high school art teacher, Michio
Kobayashi, and all my other instructors
and mentors.   —S. G.

Text copyright © 1999 by Debbie Dadey
Illustrations copyright © 1999 by Scott Goto

This story is a tall tale based on a real life.

First published in the United States of America in 1999 by Walker Publishing Company, Inc.

Published simultaneously in Canada by Fitzhenry and Whiteside, Markham,
Ontario L3R 4T8

Library of Congress Cataloging-in-Publication Data
Dadey, Debbie.
Will Rogers: larger than life/Debbie Dadey; illustrations by Scott Goto.
p.   cm.
Summary: In this tall tale, the legendary Will Rogers is so good with his lasso that he ropes
the whole earth and creates the equator and on the rebound hollows out the Grand Canyon.
Includes biographical information about the real Will Rogers.
ISBN 0-8027-8681-2.—ISBN 0-8027-8682-0 (reinforced)
1. Rogers, Will, 1879-1935—Juvenile fiction. [1. Rogers, Will,
1879-1935—Fiction.   2. Tall tales.]   I. Goto, Scott, ill.   II. Title.
PZ7.D128Wi   1999
[E]—dc21   98-35224
CIP
AC

Book design by Claire Counihan

Printed in Hong Kong
10 9 8 7 6 5 4 3 2 1